BoBSLEiGH JELLYBEANS

Illustrated by Chris Ripley

Written by Paul & Talya Shore

... for our smiley little cherub Jashia *

Printed and bound in Canada

www.ArtBookbindery.com

ISBN 978-0-9813474-0-0

Adam, Hugh, Chris, and Bobby were friends who loved to play together in the snow!

The boys' favourite game was to race their toboggans. Each day after school they would run to the park, as fast as they could, towing their sleds behind them.

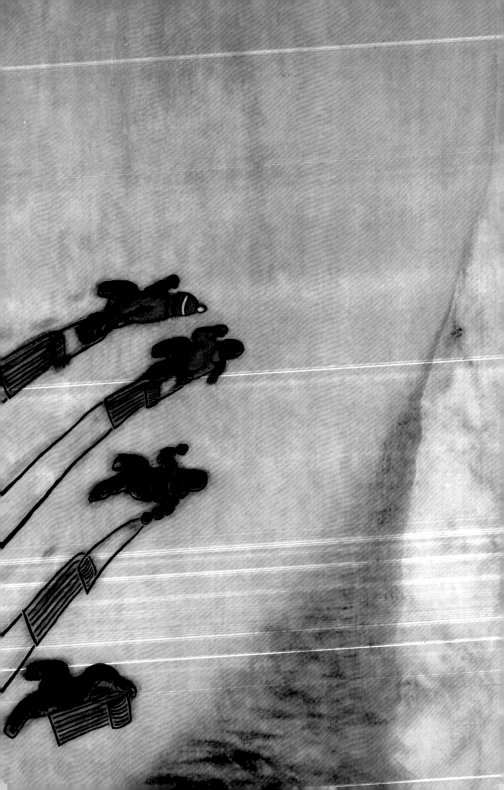

Bobby and Chris were speedy runners and always got to the hill before the others. They jumped on their toboggans and yelled, "Catch us if you can!"

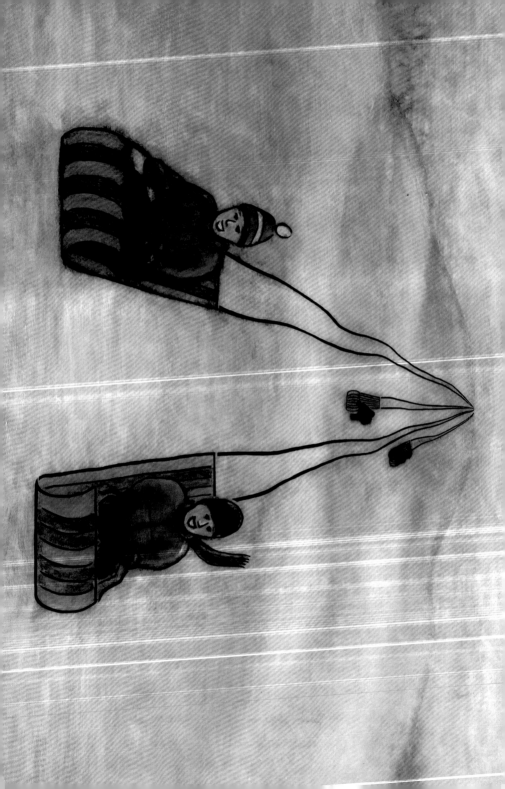

Hugh used his big strong legs to push his toboggan fast before jumping on. Soon he was catching up to Bobby and Chris.

Adam had a different style. He carefully steered his toboggan down the hill using little snowbanks to help him go faster! Soon Adam was catching up to the other boys too.

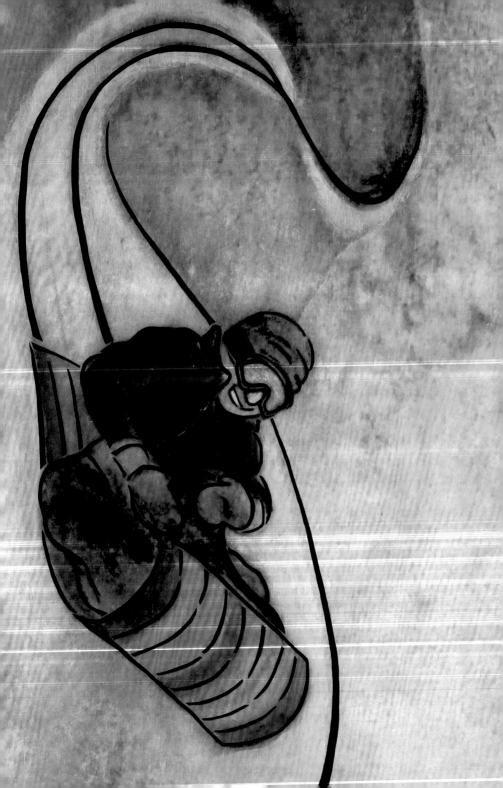

Sometimes Adam's driving skills helped him to be the first down the hill. Other times, Hugh's strength helped him to be the first. Then there were times when speedy running helped Bobby or Chris to be first. No matter who won, the boys would laugh and jump around in the snow yelling, "We are the WORLD CHAMPIONS of tobogganing!"

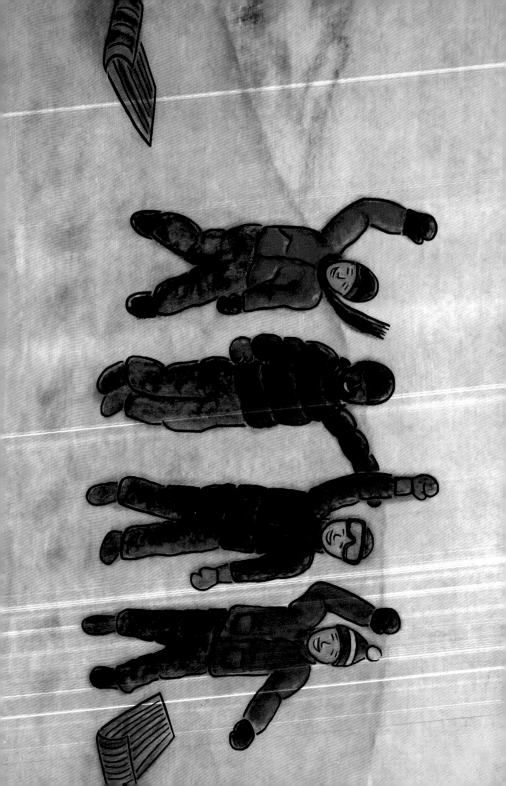

The boys would race over and over and over again, up and down, up and down --- pretending to race for Team Canada. They would play until the sun went down and their parents called them home for dinner. They never got tired of tobogganing. Zoom zoom zoom --- fun fun fun!

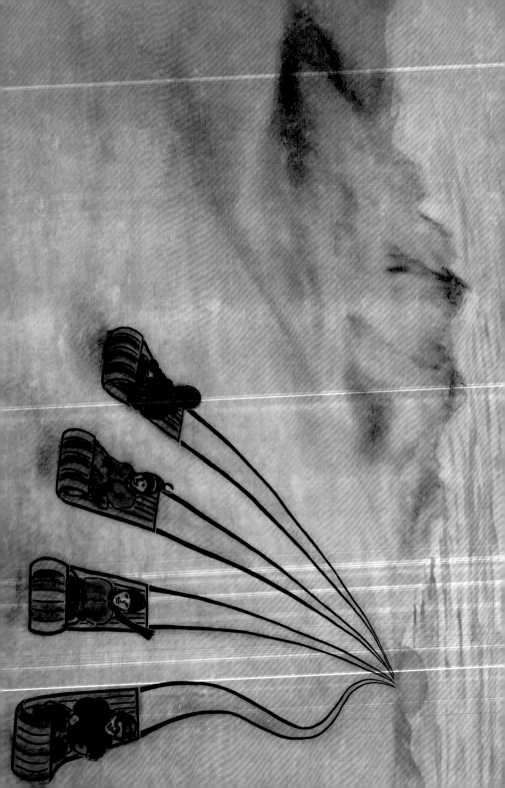

When Hugh, Bobby, Adam, and Chris grew up and became big boys, they decided to become a bobsleigh TEAM. Now they raced big bobsleighs against other teams from all around the world, just like they had dreamed of when they were children.

As a TEAM they put all their different talents together. Chris and Bobby's speed, Hugh's strength, and Adam's driving skill. They would jump into their big shiny red bobsleigh and race down the icy track with the speed and noise of a freight train!

When they first went to Whistler to practice, they met a little red-haired girl named Jashia. Jashia loved to watch them zoom down the track in their red bobsleigh with its Canadian maple leaf painted on the front. She cheered and rang her cowbell every time they raced past, "GO, GO, GO" -- clang, clang, clang.

Each time that Chris, Bobby, Hugh, and Adam would reach the finish line and get out of their sled, little Jashia would giggle. She thought their bright red race suits made them look like BIG RED JELLYBEANS!

Sometimes the guys were the fastest team in Whistler and would celebrate and yell, "We are the world champions of bobsledding!" And sometimes teams from other countries were faster and would win the races. But whoever won, Hugh, Bobby, Adam, and Chris ALWAYS had FUN! Fun just like when they were little boys racing their toboggans in the park after school!

No matter what place they finished the race in, little Jashia was always there cheering for them. "You guys are my favourite bobsleigh team! You are the FASTEST JELLYBEANS that I have ever seen!"

"Thanks Jashia!", the Bobsleigh Jellybeans would answer.

"We love hearing you cheer as we race down the track -- your happy face and cute red hair peeking out from under your toque. ALWAYS FOLLOW YOUR DREAMS and that great big smile will stay on your face forever!"

THE END

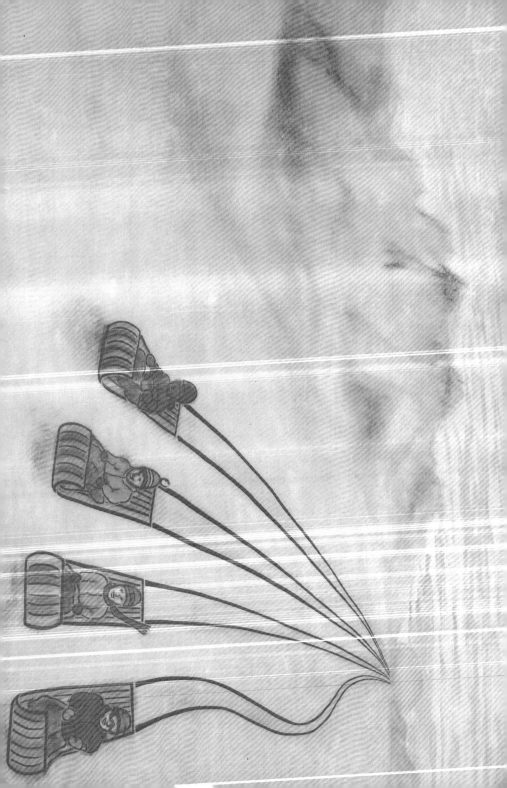

Special thanks to the entire Whistler Sliding Centre team, who have worked so hard to open a fantastic Olympic venue, and to provide Canadian athletes with a little home field advantage. And to Amanda Stepenko of the Canadian Bobsleigh team, who introduced us to Chris, Adam, Hugh, and Bobby.